THE SNOW DAY

THE SNOW DAY

KOMAKO SAKAI

SCHOLASTIC INC.

New York Toronto London Auckland
Sydney Mexico City New Delhi Hong Kong

When I woke up in the morning, Mommy said, "You can sleep late today."

"How come?" I asked, and she said, "Kindergarten's closed."

"It's been snowing all night, and the school bus got stuck."

"Snow!"

I jumped out of bed and ran for my boots.

"Wait!" Mommy said. "You can't go out until it stops snowing.

I don't want you to catch a cold."

But I snuck outside while Mommy washed dishes. I made a little snow dumpling on the balcony.

The snow hadn't stopped at lunchtime,

or later, when I had my snack.

Mommy couldn't go to the grocery store.

We played cards instead, just the two of us.

Daddy's flight got canceled, and he couldn't get home.

All of us waited for the snow to stop.

Mommy went out to the balcony.

It was cold but quiet.

No cars drove by. No one walked around.

There was just the falling snow.

"Mommy, we are all alone in the world."

Night came.

I was brushing my teeth for bed when I realized —

"Mommy! Mommy! The snow stopped!
Please can we go outside?"
"It's bedtime," she said, but then she smiled.
"Okay, just for a little while."

Mommy and I put our footprints in the fresh white snow.

We made snowballs and snow dumplings.

We even made snow monsters.

My hands froze and my nose started running.

"Oh, goodness," said Mommy. "We need to get inside!

We'll play again tomorrow."

Tomorrow . . .

Yes, tomorrow . . .

Daddy will be home tomorrow,

because it stopped snowing.

ISBN 978-0-545-31804-4

Text and illustrations copyright © 2005 by Komako Sakai.
First published in Japan in 2005 by Gakken Co., Ltd., under the title *Yuki Ga Yandara*.
All rights reserved. Published by Scholastic Inc., by arrangement with Gakken Co., Ltd.,
through the Japanese Foreign Rights Centre. SCHOLASTIC, the LANTERN LOGO,
and associated logos are trademarks and/or registered trademarks of Scholastic Inc.

Arthur A. Levine Books hardcover edition published by
Arthur A. Levine Books, an imprint of Scholastic Inc., January 2009.

12 11 10 9 8 7 6 5 4 3 2 1   10 11 12 13 14 15/0

Printed in the U.S.A.   08

First Scholastic Book Clubs paperback printing, November 2010

Design by Lillie Howard